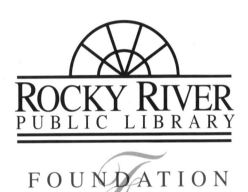

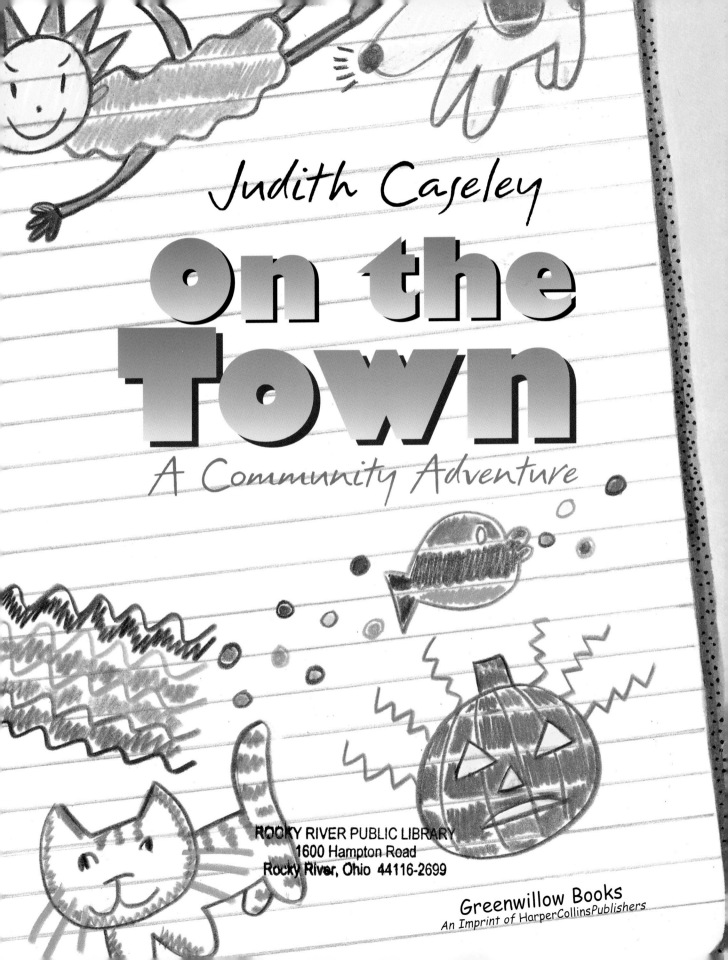

Judith Caseley

On the Town

A Community Adventure

Greenwillow Books
An Imprint of HarperCollinsPublishers

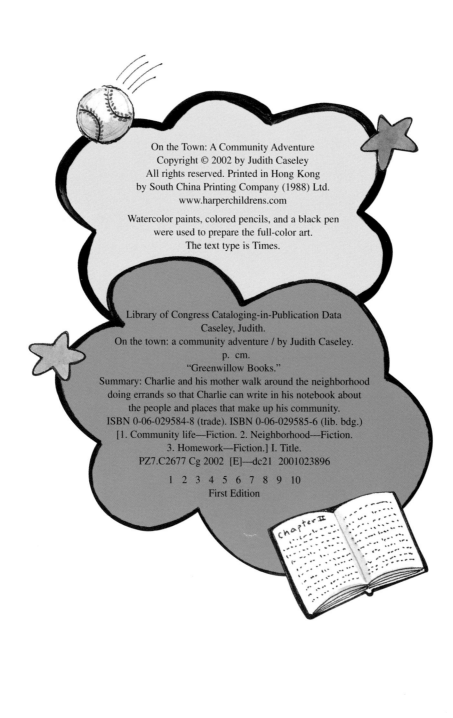

On the Town: A Community Adventure
Copyright © 2002 by Judith Caseley
All rights reserved. Printed in Hong Kong
by South China Printing Company (1988) Ltd.
www.harperchildrens.com

Watercolor paints, colored pencils, and a black pen
were used to prepare the full-color art.
The text type is Times.

Library of Congress Cataloging-in-Publication Data
Caseley, Judith.
On the town: a community adventure / by Judith Caseley.
p. cm.
"Greenwillow Books."
Summary: Charlie and his mother walk around the neighborhood
doing errands so that Charlie can write in his notebook about
the people and places that make up his community.
ISBN 0-06-029584-8 (trade). ISBN 0-06-029585-6 (lib. bdg.)
[1. Community life—Fiction. 2. Neighborhood—Fiction.
3. Homework—Fiction.] I. Title.
PZ7.C2677 Cg 2002 [E]—dc21 2001023896

1 2 3 4 5 6 7 8 9 10
First Edition

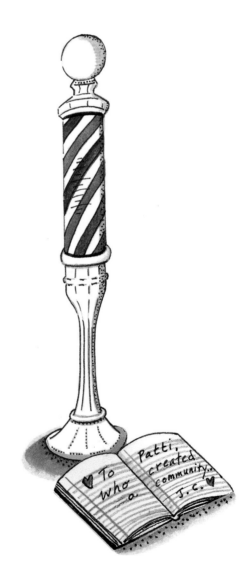

Charlie's class was studying community.
"A community," said the teacher, "is a group of
people who live or work in the same area, or who
have something in common with each other."
She gave each of the children a black, speckled
notebook. "Visit the people and places in your
community. Take your notebooks and explore."

"Homework?" asked Mama when school was over.
"Yes," said Charlie. "What is my community?"
"Let's take a walk and find out," said Mama.
Charlie's teacher left the building and waved
good-bye.
"Teacher!" said Charlie. "Should I write her
name down?"
"Absolutely," said Mama. "Your teacher is
a big part of your community."

Charlie wrote *teacher.* Then he
wrote *school* and drew pictures
of some of his other teachers.

Mama and Charlie walked through the park. The garbage
collectors were emptying trash cans. A sign on one trash
can said, "Keep your park clean."
Charlie picked up a soda bottle and threw it in the trash can
that said "Recycle." Then he wrote the word *garbage*, and
Mama spelled *collector* for him, and Charlie copied the word
recycle.

On the way into town, Charlie tripped over something.
It was someone's lost wallet, and Charlie showed it to Mama.
"Maybe we should take it to the police station," he said.

"Good idea," Mama told him, and they walked to the police station, where they met Joe the police officer and gave the wallet to him.

"You're a good part of my community," said Charlie.

"So are you," said Joe.

Charlie wrote *police station*. Then he wrote *Joe* and drew a star next to his name.

No. 707-N
Official
Police
Notebook

Police
1017

"You need a haircut,"
Mama told Charlie
as they left the
police station.

"Barber shop!"
said Charlie.
"So smart,"
said Mama.

Charlie wrote *barber shop*. Then George cut his hair, and Charlie wrote *George* and drew a pair of scissors.

"Very handsome," said Mama. "Now I need to buy stamps."

"Post office!" cried Charlie.

"My genius!" said Mama.

Charlie wrote *post office* while a lady behind the counter whose name was Evelyn sold Mama the kind of stamps that didn't need licking. Charlie wrote *Evelyn* and drew his own special stamp.

"Did you ever thank Grandma for the toy
she sent you?" Mama asked.
"We'll buy a card for Grandma at the pharmacy!"
said Charlie, writing *farmacy*.
"It's not a farm,"
said Mama,
changing the *f* to *ph*.
Then they picked out
a thank-you card, and
Charlie waved to the
man who was behind
the pharmacy counter.
Charlie wrote his name
and spelled *pharmacy*
correctly.

"I'm running out of money,"
Mama said to Charlie.
"Bank!" said Charlie.
"Bingo!" said Mama.
Charlie read the badge
on the bank teller's blouse.
Her name was Ms. Chung,
and she gave Mama money
while Charlie wrote her name
with a long line of dollar signs.

"All this hard work is making me hungry," said Charlie.
"Really?" said Mama. "And where shall we go?"
"To Henry's Luncheonette!" Charlie told her.
"Write it down," said Mama.
Then Charlie had chocolate milk, and Mama had coffee,
and Charlie drew a picture of Juanita, the waitress.
Mama pulled a book out of her pocketbook.
"Have you finished reading this?"
she asked Charlie.

"Yes! Library!" Charlie shouted.
"You're a whiz!" said Mama.

They walked down the street past the fire station. Uncle Kerry was polishing the fire engine. Charlie wrote *fire station.* He drew a fire and a hose and wrote *Uncle Kerry,* with five hearts and five stars for his favorite uncle. Uncle Kerry put a fire hat on Charlie's head and carried him around on his shoulders.

They left the firehouse and went
to the library, where they checked out some books.
Charlie wrote the librarian's name and drew a picture of her.

"It's time to meet Papa at the train,"
said Mama.
"Train station!" said Charlie.
"What a brain!" said Mama.

Papa stepped off the train and waved good-bye to the conductor.
Charlie hugged Papa. Mama kissed Papa. Charlie showed Papa his "Community" book. Then he wrote *train station* and *train conductor*, and they headed down Main Street.

"Some flowers would be nice," said Mama sweetly.

"Flower shop!" said Charlie.

"Isn't he smart?" said Mama.

Papa agreed, and Charlie drew a picture in his notebook
of the florist holding a bouquet of flowers in her hands.
Papa bought Mama a bunch of red tulips and said,
"Is anyone hungry?"

"Pizza parlor!" said Charlie.
"Sounds good," said Papa.
"Write it down while
we order," Mama
told him.

Louis
brought them
a pizza—half
pepperoni and half
mushroom—and they ate it all.
Charlie wrote *Louis* next to *pizza parlor,* and they headed for home.

Charlie played trucks with Papa.
He read books with Mama.
Then it was time for bed.

"Mama! Papa!" Charlie called
    from his room.
"What?" said Mama.
"What?" said Papa.
"I forgot," said Charlie.
"You forgot what?" said Papa.
"Community," said Charlie.
"It's all down in your notebook,"
    Mama told him.
"Not the very best part. The best
    part of all!"
"Tell us," said Mama.
"We're listening," said Papa.

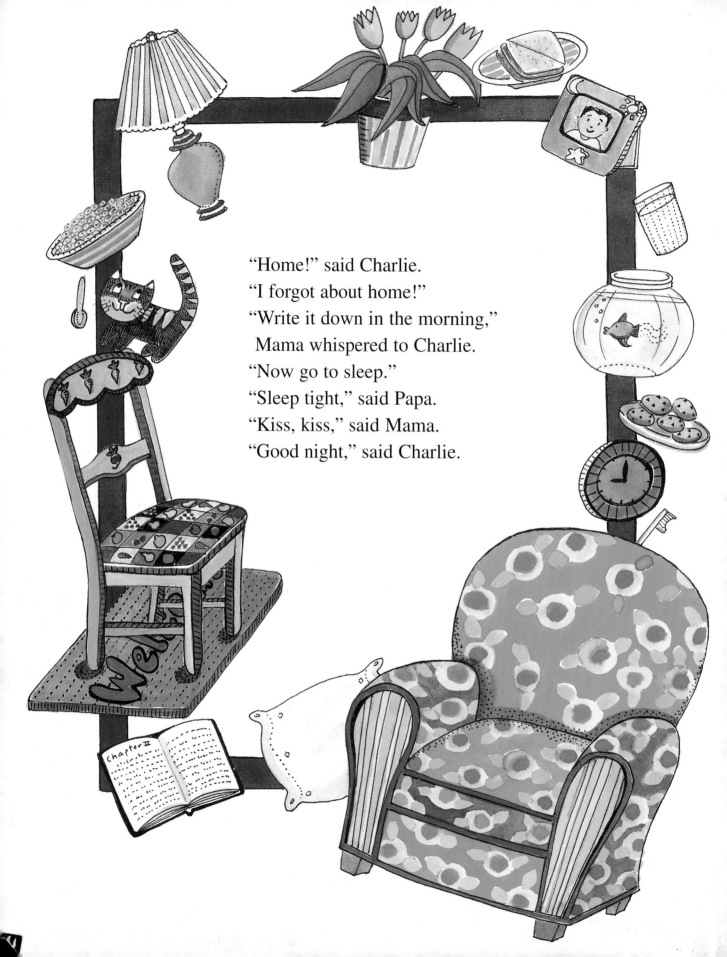

"Home!" said Charlie.
"I forgot about home!"
"Write it down in the morning,"
 Mama whispered to Charlie.
"Now go to sleep."
"Sleep tight," said Papa.
"Kiss, kiss," said Mama.
"Good night," said Charlie.

In the morning Charlie ate breakfast. He took out his notebook and sat on the porch. The mailman walked by, carrying a package. The plumber pulled up across the street. The gardener began mowing the neighbor's lawn. Charlie drew a picture and wrote the word *home*. Then he wrote *My Community* across the front of the book. His day had begun.